Karate Club

An Ivy and Mack story

T0337777

Written by Rebecca Colby
Illustrated by Gustavo Mazali
with Szépvölgyi Eszter

Collins

Who's in this story?

Listen and say

Bella

Ivy

Ms Brett

Mack

Today is karate club. Ivy goes to karate lessons with Bella.

4

Mack says, "Look Ivy, I'm cleaning the car."

Ivy says, "That's nice, Mack."

Mack looks at Ivy. She is sad.

Ivy says, "I want a yellow karate belt. Bella has got a yellow karate belt."

Mack says, "I can colour your belt yellow."

Ivy says, "Ms Brett, my karate teacher, gives us yellow belts!"

Mack wants Ivy to be happy.

It is karate club again.

Ms Brett says, "Stand up tall and look at the wall."

Ms Brett says, "Well done, Bella. Very good, Mo."

Ivy says, "Ms Brett is not looking at me."

14

Ivy kicks. She says, "Why isn't Ms Brett looking at me?"

Ivy says, "Why is Ms Brett looking at me now?"

Ivy comes home. She doesn't have a yellow belt.

Mack says, "Look, Ivy. A yellow karate belt for you."

Ivy says, "Thank you, Mack, but the yellow belts come from the karate teacher!"

It is a new lesson. Ms Brett says, "Let's try kicking again."

Ms Brett sees Ivy, but Ivy doesn't see Ms Brett.

Ivy says, "Now I want my orange belt!"

Picture dictionary

Listen and repeat

belt

karate

karate club

kick

stand

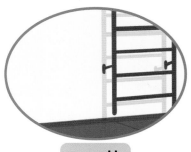

wall

1 Look and order the story

2 Listen and say

Collins

Published by Collins
An imprint of HarperCollins*Publishers*
Westerhill Road
Bishopbriggs
Glasgow
G64 2QT

HarperCollins*Publishers*
1st Floor, Watermarque Building
Ringsend Road
Dublin 4
Ireland

William Collins' dream of knowledge for all began with the publication of his first book in 1819.

A self-educated mill worker, he not only enriched millions of lives, but also founded a flourishing publishing house. Today, staying true to this spirit, Collins books are packed with inspiration, innovation and practical expertise. They place you at the centre of a world of possibility and give you exactly what you need to explore it.

ISBN 978-0-00-839779-1

Collins® and COBUILD® are registered trademarks of HarperCollins*Publishers* Limited

www.collins.co.uk/elt

British Library Cataloguing in Publication Data

A catalogue record for this publication is available from the British Library.

Author: Rebecca Colby
Lead illustrator: Gustavo Mazali (Beehive)
Copy illustrator: Szépvölgyi Eszter (Beehive)
Series editor: Rebecca Adlard
Publishing manager: Lisa Todd
Product managers: Jennifer Hall and Caroline Green
In-house editor: Alma Puts Keren
Project manager: Emily Hooton
Editor: Deborah Friedland
Proofreaders: Natalie Murray and Michael Lamb
Cover designer: Kevin Robbins
Typesetter: 2Hoots Publishing Services Ltd
Audio produced by id audio, London
Reading guide author: Julie Penn
Production controller: Rachel Weaver
Printed and bound by: GPS Group, Slovenia

MIX
Paper from
responsible sources
FSC C007454

Download the audio for this book and a reading guide for parents and teachers at www.collins.co.uk/839779